Free Rein Series

Broken

Christine Meunier

Free Rein Series
Broken
by Christine Meunier

National Library of Australia Cataloguing-in-Publication Data
Meunier, Christine
Broken
1st ed. 2017
ISBN - 978-0-244-40079-8 (pbk.)

Cover design by Metuschaël and Christine Meunier
Cover photo by Christine Meunier with thanks to Kevin Kurrle, Kisimul Farm

Foreword

I thought it was time to explore Hannah's character a little more. I feel that Jacqui and Geordie and their individual personalities have been covered better than Hannah's. And so I wanted to focus on her story in **Broken.**

I hope you enjoy getting to know her better!

Christine

Free Rein Series

1. New Beginnings
2. In Pursuit of a Horse
3. Free Reign
4. Learning to Fall
5. A Dollar Goes a Long Way
6. Contagious
7. Broken

Also by Christine Meunier

Horse Country – A World of Horses

B and B

The Thoroughbred Breeders Series

1. New Blood
2. No Hoof, No Horse
3. Recessive
4. Breakover
5. Focus
6. Yearling Sales
7. Grace

"It's obvious the author is a professional in the industry and her writing makes the novel easy to read and understand…"

"…a wide ranging caste of interesting characters giving a brilliant insight into the horse world in contemporary Australia, in particular focusing on entertaining characters who work in racing, and in a riding school. Loved it!"

"It is refreshing to read something where the horse parts ring true rather than having to suspend belief like you have to in many books and movies about horses."

"…accurate references to horsemastership…"

"…this book had appeal for both young and old. I think if you love horses, you'll like it even more. The horse aspect is right on and entertaining, particularly with the added aspect of the story taking place in Australia. I highly recommend it."

"…reading this book will inspire you!"

Praise for B and B

"…a heart-warming story that embraces her love of horses, Australia, and the outdoors… Filled with charismatic characters, you will love this story of romance and horses. Recommended reading."

"Loved this book from the very first chapter! Very well written and a great story, couldn't put it down :)"

Free Rein: Broken

One

Hannah Johnston put her hands over her ears, trying to drown out the sound of her parents' voices. They were fighting – again. It seemed to Hannah that all they ever did was work, fight and worry about money. It sure didn't make for a lot of fun times at home.

She lay back on her bed and glanced at the drawings on her wall. All of them were horses; most of them were her pony, Jasper.

She smiled as she thought about her pony. He was a lovely gelding that often beat her best friends' horses when they raced. Jacqui King and Geordie Smith also had ponies. All three of the girls kept their horses at a property titled Genesis. It was owned by Tony and Kate King, Jacqui's parents.

Geordie and Hannah spent as much time as they could on the property and with their ponies. Most of their weekends were taken up with this, although Hannah found if she went out on a Sunday morning that she was by herself. As it was, it was difficult to get a lift out there when her parents were complaining about the cost of fuel and time away from the possibility of earning money.

If she was able to get a lift with Geordie, Hannah jumped at the chance. But because her fiery friend was often at church with Jacqui, that made it very difficult.

Hannah had no doubt that this weekend would be a similar story. She was thankful that at least all three of the girls would be riding the following day which was a Saturday. It was only a week until they had their dressage day that family and friends were allowed to attend. Hannah looked forward to competing and showing off to her parents – if they came along. She had no doubt that the following day would be spent practicing their dressage tests and plaiting their ponies.

It was officially the weekend in her books – Friday night. The fact that she was home listening to her parents argue immediately put a damper on things. Having already had dinner, Hannah uncovered her ears long enough to get ready for bed. It was enough time for her to hear a little of what was going on downstairs.

"How can you justify eighty dollars for a haircut?" her father asked in an angry tone as Hannah put on her pyjamas.

"We've been over this, *Michael*. It's for work. I can claim it on tax and it was a cut, colour and style. It's important that I look my best when presenting houses to clients," Hannah's mother responded.

"Well Dianne I don't see how an eighty dollar haircut is going to convince someone to buy a house!"

"I think we really need to look at our budget again," her mother's resigned voice floated up the stairs.

"It's not going to change things! We are spending more than we're earning. We're in debt and have no way of repaying it. We need to cut back on some things and we need to do it *now*."

Dianne sighed.

"You're right. Perhaps we need to look at each other's spending and see if there are things that aren't necessary currently."

"Ok. We'd better include Hannah in this spending, too."

Hannah paused at her bedroom door as she considered going downstairs to say goodnight.

"In what way?" Dianne asked.

"Well there is spending that affects her that isn't necessary for this household," he responded, causing Hannah to sit down on the top step quietly.

There was silence for a short moment and then Hannah's mother spoke up.

"You mean with Jasper?" she clarified, causing Hannah to frown.

"Definitely. How much are we spending on agistment fees, riding lessons and Pony Club membership? None of those are *necessary* but they are regular costs. And of course there is his health care, too. It may be necessary to consider the wisdom of selling him," he stated seriously, causing Hannah to place a hand to her mouth.

She couldn't believe what she was hearing. She sat awhile longer, listening to her mother agree that they needed to look at *everything* and determine if what they paid for was

3

unnecessary, wanted or necessary. Hannah had a sinking feeling that Jasper and his associated costs were going to fall into the *unnecessary* box for her parents – even if she argued that he truly *was* necessary to her wellbeing. Not wanting to face her parents after the conversation she had just heard, Hannah went back to her room, wishing she'd kept her hands over her ears.

Jacqui King grinned as she trotted after Geordie and Hannah. The three were playing follow the leader out in the freeway paddock at Genesis. Hannah was leading and was having fun changing direction whilst using the reins in one hand, or riding without stirrups. It was a big job just to focus on what she was doing and keeping her pony Jaq under control! Still, Jacqui's mind wandered a little.

Hannah had turned up with Geordie on Saturday and had seemed very quiet. Jacqui had asked her friend if she was ok. Although Hannah claimed to be *fine*, Jacqui felt that something was wrong. She didn't feel confident to push the point though, as she and Hannah didn't seem to be as close as she was with Geordie. Whatever it was, Jacqui hoped the problem would go away soon – or that Hannah would share with them in case they could help.

For now, it was nice to see her friend focusing on her riding and enjoying herself. Already the three had practiced their dressage tests for the following week's riding club.

All of the riders in the club had a test that they had to ride for their end of year session. It was to be judged by their instructor Kara and an older gentleman named Bob who agisted at Genesis. Jacqui couldn't wait for the following weekend!

4

An added bonus was that the students had invited their parents along to watch. Geordie's were definitely coming, but Jacqui got the impression that Hannah's wouldn't. Still, it was going to be a great day.

Half an hour later the girls were removing their saddles and bridles and brushing down their mounts. They had cooled the ponies down by finishing off their game at a walk, with Jacqui in the lead. Now it was time to get their ponies comfortable before putting them out in the paddock with other agisted horses.

"Are you guys going to braid your horses for next weekend?" Jacqui asked curiously as she thought about how beautifully presented some horses were for dressage tests.

"Sure! I love doing that stuff! Mum even bought me a heap of braiding bands and a new comb," Geordie responded enthusiastically.

Jacqui grinned. Geordie was pretty laid back – even lazy – with many things, but she seemed to have a knack for plaiting and braiding very neatly.

"Maybe you could help me with Jaq," she concluded, knowing Geordie would do a better job than her.

"If we have time on the day, I'll definitely help. What are you going to do, Hannah?"

The young brunette shrugged as she continued brushing Jasper's back, deep in thought.

"I guess I hadn't really thought about it… I've just memorised my test… and I can't see my parents paying for any new grooming stuff anytime soon. I'm not even sure they'll make the effort to come along next weekend although I've given them *heaps* of notice about it."

Jacqui frowned, wondering if this was what had gotten her friend down.

"Well Geordie and I will help you braid Jasper, won't we?"

Geordie nodded as she put her grooming tools away and undid the lead rope from its quick release knot.

"All done! You guys ready to head out?" she asked, looking at her friends either side of her.

Jacqui nodded and untied Jaq, ready to follow her redheaded friend. Hannah sighed and continued brushing Jasper.

"You guys go ahead. I'm not quite done," she said quietly.

Jacqui raised her brows at Geordie who shrugged in response. When Geordie started toward the paddock that the ponies were currently kept in, Jacqui followed at a safe distance behind her. The two girls entered the paddock, closed the gate behind them and turned their ponies back to face the gate. On the count of three they undid their head collars and watched as the two equines turned around and cantered off to some other horses.

Jacqui grinned as she watched Jaq give a little buck before settling down to graze.

"I'm glad he doesn't do that with me on him!" she said, earning a laugh from Geordie.

"Agreed! Guess we'll head back to Hannah. What do you reckon is eating her?"

"She seems sad... I hope she'll share with us what's going on. We can't help if we don't know."

6

"That's true. I might just ask her."

Jacqui smiled. She wouldn't feel ok doing that, but she knew that Geordie and Hannah were closer friends and had been that way for a long time. If Geordie felt comfortable doing so, then maybe they would both know what was going on with their friend. They quickly made their way back to Hannah. Jacqui was surprised to find her still grooming, unshed tears in her eyes. Geordie stopped suddenly, having noticed the same thing.

"What's going on, Hannah?"

Hannah looked up at her two friends sadly. Tears started to fall silently down her face.

"I... last night mum and dad were having an argument about money... and they talked about having to cut back on things. Dad made the suggestion that it might be necessary to stop paying for my riding lessons, Pony Club and even agistment."

Geordie gasped.

"But where would you keep Jasper?"

"Dad even mentioned... selling him," she admitted, her tears continuing to fall.

Jacqui put a hand over her mouth. No wonder her friend was so sad!

"I can't believe they told you they might have to sell Jasper!" Geordie said, furious.

"They didn't *tell* me... I overheard them arguing about money and that was one of the things they said."

Jacqui thought about this quietly as Geordie got Hannah to repeat everything she had heard. Jacqui could

7

only see one issue – the Johnston family needed to cut back on spending. She wondered how she and Geordie could help Hannah so that it wouldn't be necessary to consider selling her pony.

"Well I know one way that you may be able to cut down on agistment costs," she cut into their conversation.

Geordie looked at her curiously. Hannah looked hopeful.

"How?"

"Do you remember when you guys first brought the ponies here and you helped mum on the property for a couple of hours a week? That helped to cover the costs of the ponies being here *and* it made the property more interesting for people to ride on."

Geordie nodded enthusiastically.

"Sure! That was great fun, but now it's more fun to ride on our ponies any time we're here."

"I agree. But it won't be fun to ride here *without* Hannah," she said soberly.

"So you're saying that we should go back to working on the property?" Geordie clarified.

Jacqui nodded.

"Sure, we all could do it. But specifically, we do it together to cut down Hannah's agistment bill. We could ask mum to give us tasks to complete each week that she feels are equivalent to the cost of agistment."

Hannah thought about this and shrugged as she put her grooming tools away.

"I guess that could work… but I don't like the idea of you guys working for *my* pony."

"Well *I* don't like the idea of your parents selling Jasper and you not being able to ride with us! I say it's a great idea, Jacqui."

Jacqui beamed at Geordie. Then she turned her attention to Hannah.

"It's one idea, Hannah. Give us a little time and I'm sure we can come up with more," Jacqui said, earning a frown from her dark haired friend.

"That's easy for you to say. Your parents *own* this place; it's not like you'll ever need to worry about paying for agistment," she said angrily, untying Jasper and heading out to the paddock to put him away.

Jacqui stared after her, shocked. She eventually turned her attention to Geordie, who was grinning.

"What did I say and why are you smiling?"

"Oh, don't worry about Hannah! She's just scared by the idea of losing Jasper and I can't blame her! We'll find a way to help. I'm smiling because you've already come up with a great idea and I'm sure you'll have more. Hannah's lucky to have you as a friend, even if she doesn't realise it yet!"

Jacqui smiled and shook her head. She sure thought Geordie's view on what had just happened was better than her own shock and hurt. She wanted to help Hannah; she just needed time to work out *how*.

Two

Jacqui listened intently to the lesson that was being shared in children's church on Sunday morning. Their teacher Brian was discussing a verse that referenced people who were poor in spirit. Jacqui wasn't quite sure what that meant, but she did know that they were said to be people who were blessed because they would be comforted. Honestly, she was confused by the whole statement.

"Who can define *poor* for me?" Brian asked as he addressed the group of children before him.

Immediately Geordie's hand shot up, causing the older gentleman to smile. He nodded at Geordie, indicating that she could provide her definition of the word.

"Someone who doesn't have a lot of money," she responded simply, earning agreeing nods from those sitting around her.

Brian's smile grew.

"It looks like many of you agree with Geordie! So let me ask you two things. One – what is *a lot*? Is it hundreds of dollars, thousands, hundreds of thousands or even millions? If it is millions, then I am well and truly poor!" he stated earning a few giggles.

"Umm... thousands or more is a lot?" Geordie responded in a questioning tone.

"Ok, so we could say that someone who is poor has less than thousands of dollars. The second thing I want to ask everyone is this: if someone only has *fifty* dollars, but they have everything they *need*, are they poor?"

This was met by silence as the group of pre-teens pondered the question. Jacqui realised if a person had food, clothes, a house and other items that they really needed to live, then perhaps the amount of money they had *didn't* determine if they were poor or rich.

"And just one more question for the moment. If I have hundreds of thousands of dollars, but I am not able to pay the rent for my home, the loan on my car, my credit card bill and my children's education because I don't have enough money, am I rich?"

This started a debate between the boys and girls sitting before Brian. He smiled and sat back, letting them debate the issue for a few moments. Eventually he clapped his hands, drawing their attention back to him.

"I'm going to leave it up to you to determine your own definition of poor. But I want to suggest that if someone is poor in something, it means they are *lacking* in that particular area or thing. Someone could be poor financially and not have enough money. Or they could be poor in good humour and always be grumpy! The verse *blessed are those who are poor in spirit, for they will be comforted* is actually referring to people who realise that *without God*, they have *nothing*.

"They recognise that they can't do everything for and by themselves – they are reliant on God to provide for them.

11

He can provide us with a job to earn money; God can help us to be wise about how we spend that money. You know what? He can even help us to study well and remember information for tests! Being poor in spirit isn't a bad thing, in fact it's humility! This is the opposite of pride and it is a *good* thing. Although many people hate the idea of being poor, being poor in spirit is not a bad thing and I encourage you all to be happy with knowing that it's important to rely on God! Now when we meet next week, I'd love to find out from *each one* of you, one thing you are relying on God to help you with. Ok?"

Each student nodded their head before they thanked Brian for the class and headed back out to their parents. Jacqui walked slowly, thinking about Brian's definition of poor and then Hannah's parents. She wondered if there was a way that she and Geordie could help Hannah to make owning Jasper less of a money issue.

"Thinking?" Geordie asked curiously as they made their way over to Jacqui's parents.

Jacqui nodded and stopped walking.

"How much are your riding lessons with Hannah?" she asked.

Geordie shrugged.

"Mum and dad pay for it... I know we have a semi-private lesson. That means it's just Hannah and I. You can have a private lesson for one person, or be in a group one which can have up to six people."

"Do you think they would all cost the same?"

"I don't think so... I think the private lesson would be the most expensive."

"Ok! Does the East Riding School have a website? Maybe their fees are on there..."

"Sure they do! But why do you want to know how much lessons are? You get *free* lessons with Kara!" Geordie stated, causing Jacqui to smile.

"Exactly! Hannah's parents can't afford all the things relating to Jasper... so I think we should make a list of them all, how much they cost and whether they're necessary... maybe we can help her – and her parents – to cut down on some costs. If Hannah could get a lesson with me and Kara for free instead of paying for one at the East, wouldn't that be better for her parents?"

Geordie grinned, nodding enthusiastically.

"Brilliant! Let's have a look online this afternoon."

Happy with that plan of action the two girls found the rest of Jacqui's family and sat down with them for a drink before going home.

"Ok, it says here that semi-private lessons are sixty dollars per lesson," Geordie said as she read from the website for the riding school she and Hannah attended.

"Is that each person, or for the two people together?" Jacqui asked.

"Each."

"Ok... and how much would you have to pay for a group lesson?"

"Ummm... forty five dollars per person."

"That doesn't seem a lot cheaper. Free sounds better to me!" Jacqui declared, earning an enthusiastic nod from Geordie.

Hannah had turned up shortly after the girls got back from church. The three had ridden together that afternoon, much like they had the day before. Still, Hannah had appeared distracted and short tempered. Jacqui didn't like her friend like this at all. She knew that with Geordie's help they had to do everything they could to fix the problem – at least as far as it related to Jasper.

The three girls had practiced their dressage tests for the following Saturday and Geordie gave Jacqui a lesson on braiding tails. Jacqui was feeling prepared and excited. It seemed the closer they got to the day however, the more distracted Hannah was becoming. That afternoon she'd forgotten the order of her dressage test and had burst into tears.

It was with some relief that Jacqui said goodbye to her friend when Hannah's parents came to pick her up. Jacqui had already organised for Geordie to stay a bit longer so they could do some research about the cost of riding lessons.

Geordie leaned over and glanced at the piece of paper Jacqui was writing on.

"So, if we count the monthly cost of agistment and the riding lessons, how much money would that save Hannah's parents?" she asked curiously.

"For a month?" Jacqui clarified.

Geordie shrugged.

"I dunno... maybe for a year?"

14

Jacqui did some quick math on her calculator.

"Just over two thousand dollars," she replied, earning a whistle from Geordie.

"That sounds like a lot! Do you think it's a lot?"

"I really don't know... I'm sure not having those costs would help, but I have no idea if it would save Jasper from getting sold. There's still the cost of getting his feet done every two months... and that's over two hundred dollars-"

"But so much better than *two thousand* dollars!" Geordie interjected, earning a smile from Jacqui.

"True, but surely saving two thousand, two hundred dollars is better than saving only two thousand?" she suggested.

Geordie frowned and sighed.

"You're right. There's no way to cut out Jasper getting his feet looked after though, that'd be cruel."

"I agree. And then if there are any vet bills, well that can be expensive and unexpected. In that way, Hannah's parents may feel it's safer to not have a horse to look after at all."

"Well that idea is horrible," Geordie responded, turning her attention back to the computer screen.

"If only she was old enough to get a job..." Jacqui mused out loud, earning a snort from Geordie in response.

Jacqui looked at her friend in surprise.

"What?"

"Well Hannah's parents work, don't they?" she said, as if that explained everything.

"Yeah…"

"But they're the ones who are saying that there's not enough money. It doesn't sound like earning money is the issue. Maybe if Hannah had a job, then they'd expect her to cover Jasper's costs and their money would just go elsewhere."

Jacqui thought about this idea, wondering if Geordie was right.

"So you're saying earning more money won't solve the problem?" she asked.

Geordie shrugged.

"Isn't it like we heard at church today? Some people can have *so much* money, but they can't pay for everything in their lives… they're poor."

"Because they don't manage what they have," Jacqui commented, nodding, "I see what you're saying. So I guess what we really should be doing is working out where Hannah can cut costs with Jasper *and* praying that her parents will see a way they can better manage what they earn."

"Bingo!" Geordie grinned, causing Jacqui to laugh.

"You know, Geordie, I think you're getting a good grasp of the lessons we're learning at church. Pretty soon you'll be teaching me!"

"Pretty sure I just did," Geordie laughed, earning a smack on the back from Jacqui.

Three

Jacqui grinned as she felt Banjo stretch his legs below her. The seasoned gelding was listening well to the aids she was giving him. Jacqui was having another riding lesson with Kara and they were once again focusing on lengthening strides within a gait.

Jacqui felt she could more easily recognise the difference between Banjo moving at a steady working trot and his lengthened medium trot. She now automatically rose higher out of the saddle when she used her legs to ask Banjo to increase the length of his stride. It felt wonderful!

"You're doing great, Jacqui! Let Banjo come back to a walk and give him a big pat. He's done a wonderful job with you."

The young girl beamed at her riding instructor.

"It seems funny that not too long ago I had no idea you could have different kinds of trot! I mean, other than a sitting and rising trot," she admitted, earning a laugh from Kara.

"There is so much to learn about horses and riding," she agreed, "I thought perhaps you'd forgotten earlier in our lesson about how sensitive they are to our focus when we ride them."

Jacqui looked at Kara in confusion as she kept Banjo moving at a steady walk around her.

"You seemed… distracted and it definitely showed as you were warming Banjo up. He wasn't sure what you wanted and a couple of times stopped, do you remember?"

Jacqui's eyes widened and she nodded her head in memory.

"I do. I was thinking about Hannah… Kara, I'm super thankful that you give me lessons on Banjo for free. I'm learning so much… and it really helps that I don't have to pay for them," Jacqui started, sitting deep in the saddle and putting pressure on the reins.

Banjo stopped obediently and Jacqui turned her full attention to the older teen.

"Do you think… would you be up for teaching someone else? I mean… I know it's already a lot that you have offered to teach me out of your own time… but would you be willing to teach me and Hannah? That is, if she could come along to the lessons you already give me?"

Kara considered Jacqui thoughtfully. Eventually she smiled and nodded.

"I am already using the time to teach you. So I think that would be ok Jacqui. But doesn't Hannah get lessons over at the East Riding School?"

Jacqui nodded.

"She does… but-" Jacqui paused, unsure how to say what she needed to without breaking Hannah's confidence.

"Does she need to stop lessons there?" Kara asked.

"I think so. Jasper is costing a little more than is good at the moment, so I've been thinking of ways that Hannah could keep doing what she wants with him, without it costing so much."

Kara nodded. She stood at Banjo's head while Jacqui dismounted.

"It's great that you're looking into other ways she can continue riding and learning, Jacqui. If Hannah is interested, then we can turn your lesson into a joint lesson with her. Would she be riding on Jasper?"

"Oh! I guess so, I know you don't really have other horses for people to ride... but would it be ok for Jasper to come onto the property?"

"I'll have a talk with my parents about that... if he's up to date on his worming and vaccinations it shouldn't be an issue. Otherwise, we can change things a bit. What if I taught you at Genesis and you rode Jaq?"

Jacqui beamed and nodded.

"That could work, too. Thanks, Kara!"

As Jacqui jogged across the freeway paddock toward her family home, she couldn't help but smile. She'd found another way to help Hannah cut down on the cost of owning Jasper. She slowed to a walk as she considered her friend's reaction to her earlier suggestion.

She couldn't understand Hannah's negative response to her idea on how to save money. It was enough to make Jacqui question if Hannah wouldn't like her new suggestion. She pondered this as she headed inside the house. She could hear her mother cooking in the kitchen and headed that way, pausing in the doorway.

19

Kate King looked up and smiled at her daughter.

"Hi, darling! Did you have a good lesson?"

"I did thanks, mum… I asked Kara about a potential change in our lessons, too. Would it be ok with you if she came over here to teach myself and Hannah in a joint lesson?"

Kate nodded as she stirred some rice on the stove.

"Sure, honey. It's the same as when she teaches everyone at the riding club. Is Hannah interested in having more regular lessons with Kara?"

Jacqui shrugged. She hesitated before replaying the conversation that she'd had with Hannah over the weekend. Kate listened intently, frowning a little.

"That sounds pretty disappointing for Hannah," she concluded.

Jacqui nodded enthusiastically.

"Totally! Geordie and I are trying to think of ways that Hannah can make owning Jasper cheaper. It'd be horrible if her parents felt they needed to sell him."

"Well not having to pay for lessons would help, but it's not the most expensive part of owning Jasper," Kate reminded her daughter.

"I know," Jacqui smiled sheepishly, "I think agistment is and I… I reminded Hannah about when she and Geordie used to help around the property to keep those costs down."

Kate nodded.

"I know we've got a lot more done on the property now... but would there still be work Hannah could do in exchange for agistment? Geordie and I could help, too... to cover the cost of Jasper's agistment."

Kate smiled at her daughter as she put some vegetables into a pot of boiling water.

"That's a wonderful offer, Jacqui. There are definitely things we could find for Hannah to do. Even some things that I do and charge agistees for, like giving hay to the horses or even picking up manure in the smaller yards."

"Great! I can't wait to tell Hannah at school tomorrow," Jacqui said enthusiastically as she headed to the bathroom to wash her hands before dinner.

Jacqui hoped that her friend would be more receptive to her help the following day.

Jacqui was keen to tell Geordie and Hannah her plans the next day at school. However, she wasn't sure she should bring it up around Caitlin and Amelia. Hannah hadn't talked about her parents or Jasper possibly needing to be sold since the Saturday when they'd ridden together.

Jacqui doubted the problem had gone away, but it seemed that Hannah didn't want to talk about it with her other friends. Still, Jacqui felt that Hannah wasn't her usual happy self. When their teacher asked Hannah to stay back before lunch, Jacqui waited outside the classroom for her. She was relieved when Geordie rushed out the door with Caitlin and Amelia.

21

Hannah talked with their teacher before leaving the classroom hurriedly, wiping at her face. Jacqui jogged after her.

"Are you ok, Hannah?"

Her friend looked at her in surprise before frowning.

"Were you listening in on me?" she asked accusingly.

Jacqui shook her head quickly.

"Of course not! I just... I wanted to talk with you and this seemed like a good opportunity."

"Ok... so what did you want to talk about?" she asked with a sigh as she slowed down to a steady walk.

"About... Jasper, actually," Jacqui said, earning a frown from Hannah.

She took a breath and continued.

"I asked Kara if you might be able to have lessons with me when she teaches me... you know, for free," Jacqui started.

Hannah stopped and looked at Jacqui, her hands on her hips.

"You told Kara about what my parents said?" she asked in a raised voice.

Jacqui shook her head quickly.

"No, I only asked if you could have lessons with me and seeing as mine were free... I asked if it would be ok for you to have them free, too..."

"And surely Kara would want to know why I would need free lessons if I already have lessons with Geordie at the East!" Hannah responded.

"She mentioned the East, sure," Jacqui started, "but-"

"I can't believe you're sharing my private problems with other people! I don't want you to talk about it anymore, Jacqui. I thought we were friends," Hannah rushed out before turning away from Jacqui and jogging toward the other girls sitting on the oval.

Jacqui stared after her, surprised and hurt. She had no idea how she could fix things. She only wanted to help Hannah, but it seemed her friend was getting upset when she tried to do that. After standing unsure for a few minutes Jacqui made her way slowly toward her group of friends. Suddenly it seemed lunch time was going to be long and uncomfortable.

Four

By the time Friday rolled around, Jacqui wasn't sure she felt up to giving Jared a riding lesson. She'd given him his first lesson on a horse the Friday before. Although it was only a week ago, she felt like things had changed a lot over the past seven days.

Last Friday she was eager to get on Jaq after he'd been cleared ok to ride. Before this, Jacqui was unable to ride him because of a virus. She'd had to practice patience though to give Jared his first riding lesson before she got on her own pony.

Then Jacqui's focus had almost solely been on her desire to practice her dressage test for their next riding club. Each of the riders in the club was performing a test to demonstrate what they'd learned throughout the year. And most of them had parents and family coming along to see them ride. Last Friday the test had been just over a week away and Jacqui was mindful of having lost time to practice on Jaq because of his illness. Now, a week later Jacqui felt confident in carrying out the test on Jaq by memory. However, her eagerness for the following day was a little lower as she thought about the possibility of Hannah not having Jasper in the near future.

She knew her friend would be riding the following day and carrying out her test on Jasper, but she wasn't sure that Hannah's parents would be coming. She wondered if they saw how much their daughter loved horse riding, if it would make any difference. *I know it can't change their money problems... but maybe it would encourage them to focus on finding a solution elsewhere, rather than selling Jasper...*

She pondered this before thinking about the lesson she'd taught the previous Friday. In spite of her shyness to teach Jared, Jacqui had found herself having a lot of fun. It had helped that Jared was a good listener and seemed to really enjoy riding Captain.

Captain was Jacqui's mother's horse and a lot bigger than Jaq. Still, his height hadn't stopped Jared from wanting to learn to ride. Jacqui reminded herself of what they'd covered the previous lesson as she got Captain ready. As soon as Jared had arrived at Genesis with Kate, he'd had a lesson with Jacqui, and then gone on to help Kate in the vegetable garden as had become habit on a Friday afternoon.

As Jacqui put on Captain's saddle and bridle, she thought back to the issue with Hannah and wondered if it was too late to insist that her parents come along to see the dressage tests the following day.

"I don't think I'd be confident enough to call and talk with them... but I think it could be really important that they see Hannah ride..." she mused out loud as she tightened the noseband on Captain's bridle.

"Who needs to see Hannah ride?" Jared asked curiously, making Jacqui look up in surprise.

"Oh! I didn't realise you were here, Jared. I was just talking to myself..." Jacqui said as she took a hold of Captain's reins and headed to the paddock with their riding arena.

Jared walked beside her, being sure to stay beside Jacqui on the left of Captain like she'd told him to. He had wanted to follow behind her previously and she pointed out how dangerous that could be if Captain got a fright and Jared was within range of his hind legs.

"Hannah's your other riding friend, right?" he asked, earning a nod from Jacqui in return.

"So why would someone need to see her ride?"

Jacqui hesitated as they walked into the 60 x 20 metre arena. She asked Jared if he remembered how to mount. He nodded.

"I think so! I need to get on from the left side, hold the reins in my left hand, put my left foot in the stirrup and hop up, making sure I don't kick him with my right foot. Oh! And I need to sit softly in the saddle so I don't hurt his back."

Jacqui beamed at the explanation.

"Great! Well I made sure the mounting block was ready for you this time," she explained, earning a grin from him in return, "so you might as well hop on."

She stepped back, staying near Captain's head in case she needed to encourage him to stand still whilst Jared got on. Captain stood quietly and Jared was quickly seated in the saddle, working to find the stirrup for his right foot. Jacqui made sure he had his reins held correctly before she encouraged Jared to start walking around the edge of the arena.

As he walked the perimeter Jacqui asked Jared to tell her what he remembered from his last lesson. She'd noted Kara do this with her and thought it was a great way to see what Jared understood without her having to do so much talking. At each letter in the arena, Jacqui told Jared to ask Captain to halt.

The big gelding stopped obediently and Jared grinned at the times when they managed to stop right next to the letters. Some they stopped a little after and Jacqui explained that he needed to *ask* Captain to stop a little sooner.

Jacqui had already set up some cones in the middle of the arena. She encouraged Jared to weave in and out of these, practicing turning left and right on Captain. They achieved this easily. As Jared turned around the last cone and headed back through them, Jacqui found her thoughts move back to Hannah. She suddenly wondered if Jared would still want to ride if he could never have a horse. He turned around the last cone and came to a stop as she'd directed.

"So… what's next?" Jared asked eagerly.

"We'll do some trotting again in a minute. I want you to walk around the edge of the arena again and rise up and down as if you were doing a rising trot, ok?"

Jared nodded and pointed Captain toward the edge of the arena.

"Jared… if you could never have a horse of your own, would you still want to learn to ride?" she asked curiously as he slowly rose up and down.

27

He nodded enthusiastically.

"That's sort of the case now, Jacqui... you see, I know mum can't afford to buy one for me... and I'm sure there are other costs involved..."

Jacqui nodded.

"Quite a few, I guess."

"So I probably won't be able to get a horse until I am old enough to work and save up for one... and even then I think I could spend my money on other things... that are more important."

Jacqui nodded as she thought about this. In time she encouraged Jared to shorten his reins and give Captain a squeeze with his legs. When he did so, the bay horse moved into a steady trot. Jared bounced for a few strides but then found the rhythm and rose up and down in time with the horse. Jacqui grinned and congratulated him as he made a lap of the arena. She then directed him to come back to a walk and to loosen his reins so that Captain could relax.

"What if... you could afford a horse and then in time... you couldn't?" she asked him.

Jared looked at her in surprise before looking back to where he was going.

"I think that would be worse than never being able to afford one," he finally said.

"Why?"

"Well you get what you want and get to enjoy it for awhile... and then it's gone. Plus, if you could have the horse because you could *afford* to and then you *couldn't*, well… it'd be really hard to deal with. And perhaps I'd be angry about it."

Jacqui nodded as she considered this. She wondered if that was why Hannah seemed so angry with her. *I get to keep Jaq and I have him at home with me… and Jasper might be gone soon and she won't have a chance to get another pony…*

"Jacqui?"

"Yeah?" Jacqui looked up at Jared.

"I asked if you wanted me to keep walking or if it was ok if I got Captain to trot again."

"Oh! Sorry, Jared… I got distracted. Of course you can have another trot."

Jacqui turned her attention to the rest of their lesson and by the end had Jared trotting between the cones, turning left and right to navigate them. By the time he'd cooled Captain down at a walk he was beaming.

"That was great, thanks!"

Jacqui blushed.

"You're welcome. I'm sorry I was a little distracted."

"Is Hannah going to have to give up her pony?" Jared asked as they made their way back to the tie up area.

Jacqui looked up at him in surprise. With a sigh she shrugged and continued walking.

"I'm not sure… but I don't really want to talk about it without Hannah's permission. She seems… angry with me at the moment and I'm trying to work out how I can make things better."

"Sometimes you can do nothing. The other person just has to deal with their disappointment and not blame someone else. And they especially can't get angry at someone who has what they want – that's not fair."

Jacqui opened her mouth to defend her friend but quickly realised that she agreed with Jared. In the end she just nodded her head.

"I still want to help in whatever way I can, but I'm not sure *how*. I was thinking that if her parents could see how much she *enjoyed* riding, that it may make a difference."

Jared shrugged as he dismounted.

"If you can't afford something, I think it doesn't matter how much someone *wants* to do it… in fact, maybe that would make things worse."

Jared put Captain's head collar on while Jacqui explained how to do so. She then demonstrated how to tie a quick release knot and had Jared practice it. By the third try he had it right. He grinned at the achievement.

"Great job! So why do you think it would make things worse?"

"Well… if my mum could see how much I would miss something because she couldn't afford to pay for it… I think it'd just make her feel sad… or even guilty. So not only could we not afford it, she'd also feel bad about it. I wouldn't want that."

Jacqui sighed and nodded.

"I guess so, thanks Jared."

"So you need to magically make horses not cost so much, ey?" he joked as he brushed down Captain.

Jacqui smiled and nodded. She then explained each brush and its role in the grooming process.

Captain wasn't that sweaty, so the rubber curry comb was only used quickly where the saddle had been sitting. Then Jared moved onto the soft body brush that was able to be used on Captain's whole body. When Jared had finished brushing over Captain he thanked Jacqui and concluded he'd better go help her mother in the veggie garden. Jacqui nodded quickly.

"Of course, you did great today Jared."

"Thanks! Oh, and Jacqui... I'm new to this church thing... but have you considered praying for Hannah?"

Jacqui stared after him as he jogged off toward the King house. She realised with a start that she'd *talked* about praying for Hannah's parents, but she'd not done so... and she had *especially* not prayed for her close friend. With a smile she realised that should have been her first step.

Five

Saturday morning indicated that it was going to be a perfect day for their riding tests. The sun was out, a few clouds dotted the sky and there was a slight breeze. Jacqui couldn't help but feel optimistic about the whole day. When Hannah turned up with her parents, she felt this was a good sign, too.

Geordie, Hannah and Jacqui quickly got to work on their ponies. They brought them in out of the paddock, tied them up and started grooming.

Jacqui groaned when she took in the sight of her grey gelding. Jaq had obviously been enjoying a roll in the dirt. His coat that was normally so close to white had brown streaks all through it. Geordie looked at him and laughed.

"Don't worry, Jacqui! He'll look so much better after a good brush. Once we're done grooming I'll give you a hand with braiding him first."

Jacqui beamed her thanks before she picked up a curry comb and started on Jaq's coat in circular motions. For every few circles that she made with the curry comb, she followed it up with a flick of her body brush, bringing the dirt to the surface of his coat and then flicking it off his body. After twenty minutes or so of brushing he looked a lot closer to his usual colour.

Needing a break from this she moved onto picking out his feet and then combing his mane. Once this was complete she decided to brush over his body one last time. By then Geordie had braided her chestnut mare Rose's tail and was ready to help Jacqui tackle Jaq's mane.

Jacqui was so focused on what she was doing that she barely registered Hannah's parents nearby. When she did focus on what they were saying, she realised with a start that most of their questions weren't about Hannah's love for riding. Instead, they were focused on asking her how often she used each item that they had paid for. And for those things that didn't appear to be used a lot, were they necessary or could they be sold?

Jacqui glanced at Hannah. She wasn't sure if her friend was more angry or upset. She was glaring at no one in particular as she brushed Jasper. Jacqui wondered if it was better that Hannah stayed silent, rather than trying to defend what had been purchased for her pony. *She* knew that anything Hannah owned was necessary to look after Jasper well, but it seemed Hannah's parents were solely focused on costs, rather than value in an item's use.

An hour later all of the riders were ready with their horses. They were groomed, tacked up and looking wonderful with their plaited manes and braided tails.

There was only one arena on the property for the riders to perform their tests in. With the varying levels of riders on the property, they didn't all have the same test to ride. Because of this, the lowest level test would be carried

33

out, working up to the highest amongst the riders. This meant that Jacqui was to ride her test first.

She was nervous about this but remembered what her mother had pointed out – as soon as she was done, she could enjoy the rest of the day and watch and learn from the others as they rode their tests. This was something she looked forward to doing in the very near future.

Jacqui had worked hard to memorise the letters in the dressage arena. Still, she was thankful that those along the perimeter of the riding area were painted in large, clear letters. They were easy to see on the ground and on horseback.

She knew that X was right in the middle of the arena. This was important because it was where she needed to halt and salute the judges. Bob and Kara were seated at the end of the arena, a little way behind the letter C. Kara had a little bell on a table beside her. She rang this, indicating that Jacqui had a minute to enter the arena and start her test.

She entered at the letter A whilst doing a rising trot. From here she had to ride to the letter X and halt. She grinned as Jaq listened to her riding aids – her legs, hands and seat – and stopped easily when she asked.

She kept her reins in her left hand, dropped her right hand to her side and lowered her head by way of salute. Then she picked up her reins in both hands and encouraged Jaq to move forward at a walk towards the letter C. From here they had to turn left and pick up a rising trot at the letter H.

Jaq obediently moved into the faster gait and Jacqui quickly checked her diagonal, making sure she was rising and falling with the outside foreleg. When they reached the letter B, which sat in the middle of the long side of the arena, they carried out a 20 metre circle at the trot before continuing along the perimeter to the letter K.

Between K and A Jacqui knew she had to canter. Because they were heading in an anti-clockwise direction, she knew that they should be cantering on the left lead and was rapt when Jaq struck out on the correct lead. They cantered until they approached the letter M and Jacqui sat deep in the saddle, applying pressure to the reins.

Jaq promptly returned to a trot just before the letter M and Jacqui brought him back to a walk when they reached H. From here they turned left and cut across the short side of the arena before turning right at the letter B. They then repeated the process of carrying out a 20 metre circle – this time on the right diagonal – and then cantering on the right lead from the letters C to F, before coming back to a trot, turning down the centre line and coming back to a walk at the letter X. Jacqui then had to halt on Jaq at the letter G and salute again.

The girl and pony pair was then free to turn at the letter C and leave the arena at a free walk. Jaq's ears were pricked forward and he eagerly stepped out in large, swinging strides as Jacqui loosened the reins and gave him a big pat. She was beaming as she left the arena.

"Great job, Jacqui! You remembered the test really well," Kate King beamed as she came up alongside her daughter and gave her leg a squeeze.

She patted Jaq on the neck too, praising the pony.

"I did, didn't I?" Jacqui asked, still grinning.

"Jaq was so good, mum! And we got both canter leads correct! I know we wouldn't have lost points for this test if we didn't, but it feels so good to know we did it *right*!"

"I can understand that honey. That was a wonderful test and now you can enjoy the rest of the day watching and cheering on your friends," Kate said.

Jacqui beamed and nodded. She accepted congratulations from her father Tony as he came over and made a fuss of Jaq. Jacqui nodded and smiled at the other riders as they came over to congratulate her. She knew that Geordie and Hannah were next to ride, so didn't grow offended when they said a few words and then rushed back to ready their ponies.

Jacqui wanted to untie Jaq's braids and brush out his mane and tail, but she didn't want to miss the other rides. Instead she quickly removed his tack; made sure he had some water and rushed back toward the arena where Geordie would be riding.

Geordie's test went well. She was carrying out dressage test stage 4, test A. Like Jacqui's it was made up of rising trot, walk and canter, except Geordie would be penalised if she was on the wrong leading leg at a canter. She also had to change her trotting diagonal in one part of the test.

Jacqui watched her redheaded friend enter the arena at a working trot, rising to the correct diagonal. Her face was serious; Geordie was obviously concentrating on the task at hand.

Jacqui gasped when Rose cantered as asked, but struck out on the wrong leading leg. Her brows rose in surprise as Geordie brought her mare back to a trot and asked again, this time getting the correct leading leg. *Wow. I don't think I would have thought to correct Jaq if he did it wrong. I would have just continued cantering on the wrong leg. I'll have to remember that for future tests.*

Apart from the one mistake at the canter, Geordie and Rose did a wonderful job. The chestnut mare moved at a steady pace throughout the whole test and changed gaits promptly when asked. The two redheaded females worked well together.

When Geordie had finished she gave a big grin and a *whoop* once she left the arena. Jacqui laughed and walked quickly over to congratulate her. She had to wait until Geordie's parents had finished, first.

"Jacqui! I know I messed up the canter lead at first, but it was an ok test, wasn't it?"

Jacqui nodded enthusiastically.

"Better than ok. And when Rose was on the wrong lead, I was surprised to see you come back to a trot and ask again. I wouldn't have thought to do something like that! But now I've seen you do it, I think I will do the same," she responded honestly, earning a large grin from her friend in return.

"We can always learn off each other. I didn't want Rose to continue on the wrong leg. I'm not sure if it was better to stop her and start again, though. I guess I'll find out when we get our test scores and feedback!"

Jacqui nodded.

"I guess I'd better let you deal with Rose and then we can watch Hannah ride."

Geordie nodded, waved goodbye and trotted off on her mare toward the tie up yards. Jacqui watched her go before turning her attention back to the arena. Hannah was waiting on Jasper, her attention on her parents. They seemed to be arguing about something and Jasper was getting agitated. Jacqui could see that Hannah wasn't happy, either – and it was getting communicated to her pony, loud and clear.

"I hope she's able to focus on her test, rather than her parents when she rides," Jacqui murmured to herself.

"She doesn't look too happy," Geordie whispered as she came up beside Jacqui.

Jacqui shook her head.

"No... I thought it was going to be a good thing for Hannah's parents to be here... but now I'm not so sure. I really thought if they saw her ride and saw how much she *enjoyed* it..."

"I know me too. I think they're too focused on their own problems and they don't even realise that one solution they're considering is going to create a whole other problem for Hannah."

Jacqui looked at Geordie curiously.

"You're right! We can't really say anything though, can we?"

Geordie shook her head.

"Not us... but maybe someone can," she said cryptically.

Jacqui didn't get the chance to ask what she meant by that. Kara had rung the bell and Hannah was due to enter the ring.

Six

Hannah had Jasper moving forward at an energetic trot as she entered the ring, heading down the centre line towards the judges at the end. Jasper obediently stopped in the middle of the arena where the letter X was located. Hannah dropped her right hand and bowed her head in a salute. She then picked up her reins in both hands and started her test. Jacqui grinned and glanced over at Geordie.

"A great start!"

Geordie nodded distractedly, her focus on their other friend in the arena. Hannah moved off at the walk and picked up a working trot again at the letter G.

She turned left at the letter C and started her 20 metre circle. Jacqui frowned as Jasper's trot slowed, his ears flicking back and forth. She glanced at Hannah as the gelding came back to a walk. What was going on?

"I don't understand-" Jacqui started as Hannah pushed Jasper into a trot again.

"I think she's forgotten what's next and gotten distracted! Jasper wasn't sure if he should keep trotting."

Concerned, Jacqui watched as her friend came out of the 20 metre circle and continued riding, a frown on her face. It seemed she remembered – a little too late – that she was supposed to be cantering somewhere between the letters A and F. Jacqui sighed as the pair picked up a canter a little after F.

"At least Jasper is on the correct lead."

"Humph, she looks really angry," Geordie muttered her eyes still on Hannah, "I hope she remembers the rest of the test."

The girls continued watching whilst Hannah completed her dressage test. Although she carried out the rest of it correctly, Jasper's movements were hesitant a lot of the time and his ears kept on flicking back to his rider. Jacqui thought it looked like he was asking Hannah for some confirmation that he was doing the right thing.

"Poor Jasper looks confused!" Jacqui whispered as Hannah left the arena.

Jacqui could see that her friend was trying to hold back tears.

"I think he's not the only one," Geordie muttered as she started to walk after Hannah.

Both girls assumed their friend would head back to the tie up area and unsaddle the bay gelding. Instead she pointed him toward the house paddock and took off at a trot, then a canter. Jacqui turned to Geordie in surprise. Her friend shrugged in response.

"Maybe she just wants to be alone? I think she's probably frustrated... and a little embarrassed. She had that test well memorised."

"Do you think we should go after her?" Jacqui asked, watching as their friend got further away on her pony.

41

Geordie shrugged, surprisingly unsure what to do. The two girls lingered by the arena, not certain what they should be doing next. There were still a couple of riders to carry out their tests in the arena. Soon Kate King and Hannah's parents were with Jacqui and Geordie.

"What was that all about?" Kate asked curiously, her gaze on Jacqui.

The young blonde shook her head and raised her shoulders in a shrug.

"I think she's really upset, mum. We're not sure if we should go after her or not."

"I'll go," Michael Johnston declared, strolling toward the gate to the house paddock.

Jacqui and Geordie watched him go before turning their attention to the two mothers. In the background one of the older girls was carrying out her dressage test.

"Oh dear, I guess this will just confirm for Michael that Jasper isn't worth the investment," Hannah's mother Dianne said, causing Jacqui to gasp in surprise.

Geordie shook her head emphatically.

"Actually, it's just showing how much Hannah is going to *lose* if you sell him!" she ground out angrily, turning on her heel and walking away.

Kate raised her brows in surprise. Jacqui felt herself growing red as she looked at the two older women before her.

"Sorry... I'm not sure Geordie should have said that," she whispered as Kate placed a hand on her shoulder and gave it a reassuring squeeze.

"I'm not sure I understand what Geordie was saying, dear," Dianne said as she looked at Jacqui.

Jacqui looked at the other woman before turning her gaze to her mother, her brows raised in question. Kate nodded for her to speak. Jacqui sighed.

"Hannah... overheard that you guys were thinking it would be better to sell Jasper than keep him... and have to deal with the costs of owning him. I think she's been so worried about that that she's gotten distracted and just did a bad test. Normally she's really good at this stuff. She's just so upset by the idea of losing Jasper... and horses are sensitive animals. They can feel when their rider is upset or confused... and it can make them just as confused."

Dianne raised her brows in surprise.

"I didn't realise that Hannah's emotions could affect her horse. Nor I guess had I realised how much Jasper means to her... Michael and I do need to cut back on our spending in a lot of areas, but maybe..."

"Yes?" Jacqui asked curiously, eager to hear that there was a solution other than selling Jasper.

"Oh, nothing. I hope that Michael is able to calm Hannah down and that we haven't ruined the day for everyone," she said suddenly, dashing Jacqui's hopes.

The young girl sighed and headed after Geordie. She didn't see how the conversation was going to work out for Hannah. She left her mother talking with Dianne as she headed back to where Jaq and Rose were munching on grass in their respective yards.

Hannah was surprised when she heard footsteps behind her. Even more unusual was the fact that they sounded like her father's heavier walk than that of either of her friends. What did he want?

She had brought Jasper to a halt in the middle of the paddock and loosened her reins. She had no fear that he would take off on her and was happy to let him eat the grass below – even if he did still have a bit in his mouth. Hannah was too upset to be concerned about encouraging a bad habit. She sat quietly, wiping at her eyes as she thought about the horrible test she'd just done on her pony. She didn't acknowledge her father's presence, but knew when he came up beside her and laid a hand on Jasper's neck.

"Do you want to help me understand what's going on?" Michael asked bluntly as he looked up at her.

Hannah wasn't sure that either of her parents understood her passion for horses at this point in time. She did appreciate her father's direct way of talking, however and felt this helped them to be closer than she was with her mother. If her father didn't understand, he said it and waited for her to explain, rather than trying to guess what was wrong like her mother did. Hannah sniffed and wiped at her eyes again.

"I'm upset because I just rode a really bad test. At a time when I should be cherishing every last moment I have with Jasper, I'm being sad and confused and making him confused and messing up *everything* when I ride him."

"I don't know a lot about riding horses, Hannah but I don't think you messed up *everything* when you just rode that test. It seemed pretty similar to Geordie's test," he commented, causing her to shrug.

"Jasper walked when we were supposed to be trotting because he got mixed signals from me – I forgot what was next. And then later we cantered too late."

"But you did get him to trot again, didn't you?" Michael asked gently.

Hannah nodded.

"And you did canter, even if it was later than expected, yes?"

Hannah shrugged.

"I guess."

"We all make mistakes, Hannah. The important thing is how we deal with them."

"So… I should not be upset and just enjoy the rest of the time I have with Jasper?"

"You're speaking like that time is about to run out very soon," Michael commented, holding her gaze.

Hannah looked down and played with the mane at the base of Jasper's neck. She glanced back at her father.

"Isn't it? I heard you and mum talking…"

Michael sighed.

"As I said, Hannah, we all make mistakes; some of them larger than others. Unfortunately, your mother and I have made the same mistake over a long time – we have allowed our spending to be more than we are earning. And now we have to make some drastic changes to fix the problem."

"Like selling Jasper," Hannah whispered, looking out across the paddock.

45

"*Like*, yes," Michael said solemnly.

A sob escaped from Hannah's throat as she closed her eyes and the tears fell. Her father reached for her hand.

"I said *like* selling Jasper, *not necessarily* selling Jasper. We may need to go see a financial advisor, but I am sure there are other areas where we can cut costs. We may need to stop the non essentials with your pony for awhile – like riding lessons and this riding club, but I don't think we need to think about selling him," he said slowly.

Hannah stared at her father, thinking over what he had just said.

"So… you won't sell him?"

"I can't make that promise yet, Hannah. But I will honestly say that I'll do whatever I can to make that not happen. Until your mother and I have reassessed our whole budget and spoken with a financial advisor, I'm not going to guarantee anything. But please know that your mother and I don't want to take Jasper away from you."

Hannah sniffed and nodded. Michael gave her hand a squeeze before glancing back to the arena paddock where things were finishing up. The last rider had just completed their test.

"It looks like it may be home time," Michael commented quietly.

Hannah nodded before cringing.

"Do you think… we could make our way back slowly? I don't really feel up to facing everyone at the moment."

Michael smiled.

"Why don't you tell me all about this property as we make our way back at a walk?" he suggested, causing Hannah to smile in return.

She nodded and started to tell Michael about the names of the paddocks and what had been added to them – sometimes with her, Geordie and Jacqui's help. Michael listened intently.

Jacqui sighed as she lay down for bed that night. It had been an eventful day! She felt funny that she hadn't had a chance to talk with Hannah after her ride, but was thankful that at least Hannah's parents were aware of how sad she'd grown at the idea of not having Jasper. Jacqui remembered with a start that she still needed to pray for her friend. She closed her eyes quickly before speaking quietly.

"God, thank you for my friend Hannah and her pony Jasper. If it's at all possible, Lord, I would love for Hannah to be able to keep Jasper. I know it's not smart to have a horse if you can't afford to look after it well... but, I think that maybe it could be possible for Hannah to keep Jasper *and* for her parents to spend less on him. Help me to become aware of more ways that Hannah can save money whilst still getting to enjoy owning and riding Jasper. Amen."

Jacqui lay in her dark room, replaying the day's events in her mind. She was pleased and excited that she'd successfully completed her first dressage test on Jaq. She was also proud of how well they had worked together and how great he looked turned out with plaits in his mane and a braid in his tail. She was thankful for Geordie helping her to learn that new skill!

47

Jacqui knew that each of them would have to wait a little while for feedback from their individual tests. Although Kara and Bob had scored them whilst they were riding, the individual scores and feedback would be presented to them at the next riding club which would be in the New Year.

Kate had agreed with Jacqui that night that the day had been a success. Most of the riders had parents attending to watch them and Kate and Tony had received lots of compliments with regards to what they were doing at Genesis.

When Jacqui had voiced her concern about not getting to talk with Hannah before she left, her mother assured her that the following afternoon after church – or even Monday at school would be soon enough for her to touch base with her friend. Jacqui assumed – and hoped – that Hannah would be about to ride the following day. She was keen to know that everything was ok or rather, *if* everything was ok.

Kate told Jacqui that she'd had a good chat with Hannah's mother and the pair had discussed possibilities regarding changing their financial situation. Jacqui guessed this was a good thing.

Just before Jacqui drifted off to sleep, she pictured herself, Geordie and Hannah playing *follow the leader* on their ponies like they had many times before. She didn't want that to change.

Seven

Brian looked around at the group of students before him. He gave them a smile and introduced their topic for that Sunday's lesson.

"Today I want to talk to you about someone who is broken or broken hearted, as the bible often puts it. We read in Psalm 34:18, 'The Lord is near to the broken hearted; he delivers those who are discouraged.' Is someone able to describe broken or broken hearted for me?"

Jacqui thought about this for a moment. Hannah's name came to mind and she frowned. What was that about? She realised with a start that Hannah seemed broken. She raised her hand hesitantly.

"Yes, Jacqui?"

"Well… when something – or someone – is broken… they aren't what they used to be… or what they should be? Or… a piece of them is missing," she responded, a question to her tone.

Brian nodded as she spoke.

"That's a great explanation! Let's think of a simple example – a mug. If it's broken, it may be in more than one piece, or have something missing. If our mug is missing its handle or there's a hole in it and our drink comes out, it isn't doing what it was made for, is it?"

The students shook their heads, agreeing that it wasn't.

"But what about a broken person?" Geordie asked curiously.

Brian smiled.

"I actually believe it's the same! *Each one* of us is made to contribute to this earth. We are here to *add* to it; to make it better! When we're broken because of loss, hurt or something else, we don't function as we normally would. And so we are no longer contributing in the way that we should... the world isn't as good as it could be, because we're so focused on being broken..."

Brian let the children focus on that for a moment before he asked them if they remembered what had been covered the week before. One of the boys raised his hand. Brian nodded at him.

"Go ahead, Joe," he encouraged him.

"We discussed the definition of poor and learnt that being poor in spirit is ok, because God will comfort us. Even if we had all the money in the world, we would be poor if we didn't have God."

"Great! Thanks, Joe. I want to suggest another thing we will be if we don't have God in our lives – broken. We may be disappointed by things in life, but God can comfort us when we are *and* He can make things turn out for our good. But if we aren't aware of God, it can be difficult to be comforted by Him!"

Brian looked around at each of the students as they considered what he had just said. He smiled at them.

"Now I have a little task for you guys this week. I want you to think about someone in your life who may seem broken hearted. Perhaps they've lost hope about something; maybe they are sad because of something that has happened. Maybe it's even *you* who comes to mind. I want you to pray for that person to be encouraged by God! If they don't know Him, they may not realise that it's God who is helping them; but that doesn't mean He can't! Can you all think of someone for me and pray for that person, starting tonight?"

As the students nodded their agreement, Brian continued talking.

"Great! Next week I'd love to talk about anything incredible that may have happened for the person you've been praying about. I'll look forward to hearing from you! Now before we finish for the day, I'm pretty sure you each need to tell me what one thing you were relying on God to help you with recently. Who wants to go first?"

Geordie came back to the King's for lunch and the girls quickly started planning what they would do with their afternoon. It was a beautiful day and they knew one thing was an absolute: they would go riding.

Both girls had assumed that Hannah would be riding with them, but neither had checked that was the case. They were both equally surprised and disappointed when their friend hadn't turned up by the time they had caught, groomed and tacked up their ponies. Jacqui wondered if it was worth waiting.

51

"Let's ride. If Hannah turns up, we can always help her get ready quickly; our ponies are already done," Geordie reasoned.

With a shrug Jacqui mounted Jaq and followed her friend into the house paddock. The two were planning to warm up with a game of follow the leader and then do some jumps. Geordie quickly decided it would be better to do their warm up as if they were riding in pairs.

"This way we can talk easily!" she reasoned.

Jacqui grinned.

"That's true. Do you think we should call Hannah tonight?" she asked curiously.

"I think so. I know we'll see her at school tomorrow, but it would be good to talk to her before then... I did ring last night," Geordie admitted, surprising Jacqui.

"You didn't say! How is she?"

Geordie shrugged.

"I left a message with her parents. They said she was busy and she never called me back."

"And you still think we should call her tonight?" Jacqui asked with an unsure tone.

"Sure! In fact, I think *you* should call her; she hasn't returned my call. She doesn't have to talk to us, but I think it's good that she knows we've been asking how she is and wanting to talk to her."

Jacqui wished she had Geordie's confidence to look at the situation that way. She knew that her friend knew Hannah a lot better than she did, but she didn't think it was likely that Hannah would want to talk to *her* instead of

52

Geordie. She felt quite the opposite, especially when she considered the recent conversations she had had with her friend.

"I'm really not sure she'll want to talk to me, Geordie," Jacqui said as they continued walking on their ponies.

"But you won't know unless you call, will you?" her friend countered, "The worst that can happen is she's not available and her parents tell you she'll call back, then she doesn't! Now let's trot."

Geordie squeezed Rose with her calf muscles and the chestnut mare stepped out into the faster gait eagerly. Jacqui let her get a few horse lengths in front of her before she asked Jaq to do the same. She thought maybe Geordie was right, she *should* just call Hannah. But a part of her wondered if doing so would provide another opportunity for her friend to get annoyed with her. She didn't want that at all.

As she trotted along on Jaq she decided she would do two things that night. The *first* was to pray for Hannah and the situation with Jasper. The second would be to call her friend to see how she was doing.

Kate glanced at her husband as the phone rang late on Sunday evening. The kids had recently gone to bed and she wasn't expecting any calls. Tony shrugged his shoulders as if to say he had no idea who it could be, either. She rose from the couch and headed to the phone, picking it up on the third ring.

"King residence, Kate speaking."

53

"Oh, I'm glad it's you Kate! I hope this isn't a bad time to call... it's Dianne, Hannah's mother," a voice gushed out on the other end.

Kate smiled.

"Hi Dianne. I'm free to talk, is Hannah ok?"

"Oh, yes! Well, physically, yes... emotionally I'd say she could be better and in a way... that's what I wanted to talk to you about..."

"Yes?"

"Well, yesterday at the riding club I think you mentioned your role in your job related to finance and budgets?"

"That's right. It's a part time role, but I oversee what comes in and goes out and make sure we're on track with what we have budgeted to spend."

"That's what I thought! Michael and I know that we need to speak with someone about our finances. And honestly, we have got an accountant... but I am a little hesitant to spend more money when that's the issue in the first place. Although I know he may be able to help us determine a course of action..."

Kate nodded on the other end of the line, wondering if Dianne was angling for her to have a look at their finances to help them not incur extra costs that they couldn't afford. She glanced at Tony sitting on the couch, watching her.

"Dianne, would you like me to go over your budget with you? I have a simple spreadsheet that we could use to see how your whole financial situation is looking," she suggested, noting her husband's grin in the room next door.

"Would you? Oh, that'd be wonderful! I know the overall problem, but maybe you can help me to identify areas where we can cut back or save money… especially if it means we don't have to sell Jasper. Poor Hannah is devastated by that idea."

Kate smiled as she thought about Jacqui's bond with Jaq.

"I can understand that, Dianne. I know of another little girl who would feel the same if that had to happen to her pony. In fact, Jacqui has been working on a list of ways that owning Jasper could be *less* expensive. I'll get her to write them down for you," Kate responded.

"Oh! Hannah didn't mention any of that; that's wonderful! When would you be free to get together? I can juggle things at work if need be."

"How about you come around tomorrow afternoon or evening? We can have a cuppa and see how things are positioned regarding your finances."

Dianne quickly agreed, determining an exact time with Kate. In spite of work and having to get dinner ready for each of their families, the two women determined late afternoon would work for an hour or so. Kate said goodbye and hung up the phone. She wandered back into the lounge room and laughed at her husband's knowing smile.

"Kate King to the rescue!" he teased.

Kate shook her head.

"No, honey; God given skills and some prayer to the rescue. Let's go to bed and be sure to pray about the Johnston's situation. Hopefully I can shed some light on things for them tomorrow *without* it costing them a trip to the accountant. If not, I'll be sure to advise them that should be their next move!"

Tony nodded his agreement, stating that financial help was one area that shouldn't be cut back on. He switched off the light and followed his wife to their bedroom.

Eight

Jacqui contemplated the previous morning's message at church as she brushed over Jaq. The afternoon was looking unusually gloomy for a summer's day and she wasn't sure if she wanted to risk riding and getting wet. Dark clouds had gathered over the property, sitting so low she felt she could almost touch them. *It makes me feel sad just to look at them.*

Perhaps it was the weather that had led to the lack of horse owners on the property that afternoon. Jacqui knew that during the day people wouldn't likely be around as most of the riders were of school age. That said, there was often one or two people about each afternoon and the weekends were especially busy with horse owners visiting, riding their horses and catching up. Jacqui was surprised to see old Bob pull up in his vehicle and slowly make his way out of the car. He had a head collar and lead rope in his hand and made his way straight to the paddock that held his grey warmblood mare, Venetian.

Jacqui's thoughts soon turned to Hannah and what was troubling her. She thought about this as she picked out Jaq's feet. Whether or not she was going to ride, she knew it was important that she groomed his *whole* body. This would help her to notice anything that was out of place. She knew that grooming was good for Jaq's coat, but it also helped her to bond with him and find any cuts, scrapes or other issues that may need tending to.

"Afternoon, little lady. How are you today?" Bob asked as he walked Venetian into the stall next to Jaq.

He turned her around and clipped a lead rope to either side of the mare's halter, cross tying her. The big grey mare stood quietly, looking out at the property before her. Jacqui smiled at Bob after finishing Jaq's feet.

"Hi. I'm ok, I guess. How are you?"

"I'm well! But your answer didn't sound very convincing. What's troubling you?"

Jacqui shrugged as she put her hoof pick away and pulled out a metal comb for Jaq's mane.

"I am good, really. I'm just thinking about a friend who is having some troubles. I'm not sure how I can help her so that things will be better."

Bob nodded as he pulled a carrot out of his jacket pocket and broke it into pieces. Venetian's ears pricked forward at the sound and her attention was focused on her owner. Bob held out a piece of carrot on his palm, his fingers flat as he offered her the treat.

"Sometimes we need to learn that we can't fix every problem. We can't always fix our own problems and shouldn't feel that we have to fix other peoples' problems, too!"

Jacqui nodded.

"I know... I just wish I could."

"And that's a wonderful wish, Jacqui. As long as it doesn't get you sad in the process. You can do everything you can for your friend, but you have to be content knowing that for all you *can* do, it may not solve things completely. And to be honest," his voice dropped to a whisper, "it's not your job!"

Jacqui smiled as she thought about this.

"That's true... are you going to ride today, Bob? It looks like it's going to rain."

"It does! But water won't make me shrink," he commented, causing the young girl to smile.

"I guess not."

"Besides, riding in all sorts of weather is good training for horses! Although Venetian was broken in well, it is my job to keep her responding well to a variety of situations."

"Broken in? What's that?" Jacqui asked curiously.

"Well I think these days the correct term is *started under saddle*. Back in the *old days* when horses were introduced to being ridden, it was often referred to as being broken in. I think the reference is to having to break their spirit – to get them to recognise man as their master and in control."

Jacqui cringed.

"That sounds terrible!"

"I agree, Jacqui. And the way it was done by some forceful people was not nice at all! Today there are a lot gentler ways to get a horse to accept a saddle – and a rider – on their back. You see, the horse is a prey animal. This means that in the wild they have predators that would jump on them and try to harm them so they could have a meal."

Jacqui nodded for Bob to continue.

"Although a lot of horses are now domesticated, they still have a reaction of fleeing from any perceived danger. That is, if they think they are going to be jumped on, they are likely to run away! That's what makes humans riding horses so incredible. They *trust* us to hop on their backs. But when horses were first introduced to being ridden many years ago, they were forced to have people on their backs. They didn't do it because they trusted us, but because they were fearful of what would happen if they *didn't*."

Jacqui cringed as she thought about this.

"It sill sounds horrible."

"I agree. Now more people feel that it is better to teach the horse to trust us first, *and then* to find a way to get a saddle on their back and eventually a person. The horse learns that it can trust humans and that it is more comfortable to be ridden, than it is to be away from the human or not do what they want."

"So people still make horses uncomfortable if they won't allow us to ride them?"

"In a way, yes. But it's more often through causing the horse to be constantly moving and when they quietly accept the saddle, they can rest. So they often choose to take the saddle, rather than be made to work," Bob explained, causing Jacqui to smile.

"So you're saying horses are lazy?" she questioned, causing him to laugh.

"One person may say lazy, another may say clever. Either way, it means that we can introduce a horse to the idea of being ridden with a saddle on, without pushing them around physically."

Jacqui agreed that this was a good thing.

Kate set down a cup of coffee before Dianne and pulled up a chair, her laptop already on. A spreadsheet was open with some columns already filled in.

Dianne had a pile of papers before her, most of these bills. Kate tried not to cringe at the *overdue* notice on a couple of these. She was thankful that she and Tony had already prayed about this meeting, but sent up another quick prayer that God would guide her as she tried to help an acquaintance. Dianne also had a notebook and pen beside her, with a few ideas jotted down. They related to how the Johnston's felt they could cut back on money in some areas.

Dianne sipped on her coffee as she glanced at the spreadsheet on the screen.

"So... the first column is for expenses and this is broken down into a weekly amount?" she asked, reading over the various columns.

Kate nodded.

"I would guess you're the same as us. Some months we have a lot more bills than we'd like! Like if gas, electricity and water bills all fall on the same month... Other months we may have no bills due. The weekly amount helps us to keep an idea of how much we should be putting aside regularly to help cover the bills when they *do* all come in at once," she explained, noting Dianne's brows raise in surprise.

"Well! We just tend to make do and pay bills off as they arrive, based on what we've earned that month. It varies for us because I earn a commission."

Kate nodded slowly as she thought about a way to tactfully encourage Dianne to plan a little more.

"Do you have a base wage, Dianne? A minimum amount that you *know* you will earn each month?"

The other woman nodded.

"Ok. Can you write that down for me? I think we should work with that figure... we can consider your bonuses later."

Dianne did so before glancing back at the screen. She frowned when she came to a column that she didn't understand.

"You've got a column there titled *tithe*. What's that for?"

Kate smiled.

"A tithe is technically a tenth of what we earn. But it's there because we give this percentage into our church. It's a way for us to give back to God because He's blessed us with the ability to earn income."

Dianne considered this quietly, sipping on her coffee again.

"But wouldn't you be better off if you saved this money and earned interest?"

"No," Kate responded simply, causing the woman to frown.

She smiled softly.

"I'll try to explain, but first I should say that we use this percentage to guide us on saving, too. We give a tithe into our local church and we *save* a tithe. So we already know that at least 10% of what we earn goes into savings. But Tony and I have a philosophy that we feel is tried and true. *First* we give back a little to God and then we trust him to help us use the rest wisely. We have weeks that are hard, sure. But we've never gone without. In fact, most of the time we have *more* than we need. And I truly believe it's because of how we prioritise our finances."

This caused the other woman to sit quietly. Kate concluded the conversation was either giving her a lot to think about, or it was making her uncomfortable. She placed the cursor in the first column of the spreadsheet.

"How about we start with expenses! I can fill in details based on the bills you've brought today," she suggested.

Kate wanted Dianne to be able to think about what she'd said without interruptions. Hannah's mother nodded and handed over the pieces of paper so that Kate could start to fill in the spreadsheet.

Over the next hour the two women were able to get an overall picture of the Johnston's finances. Both could clearly see that more money was going out than was coming in. Kate was able to suggest ways that regular bills could be lowered through pay on time discounts and paying annually rather than monthly. Dianne furiously made notes as Kate listed different ways for them to make the same amount of money stretch further.

Because time was pressing for the two, Kate printed out the spreadsheet and handed it to Dianne, suggesting she talk with Michael about it. She knew that the two of them had to work together to turn the financial situation around.

Before Dianne left Kate was sure to give her the list that Jacqui had put together regarding Jasper, too. The other woman smiled her thanks as she read the list of points. She told Kate that they were simple, effective ideas and she was really thankful for Jacqui's help. On a whim, Dianne gave Kate a quick hug before she raced out the door, dodging puddles in her high heels.

Kate smiled as she waved goodbye, watching the flashy car make its way down the driveway as the rain drizzled outside.

"I hope they can turn things around, Lord... help them to discover a heart for what's necessary and to learn to let some of their *wants* go if it's going to cause them strain financially," she prayed quietly as she watched her daughter across the property putting Jaq back in his paddock.

Nine

Jacqui was surprised to find Hannah waiting at the classroom door the following morning for school. She was further amazed when her friend smiled once she saw her. She wondered what had caused the drastic change from Monday's behaviour. Hannah had answered her curtly if spoken to but otherwise had ignored Jacqui and Geordie. She'd spent most of the day not talking to anyone and the girls had decided to leave her be. They weren't sure how to fix things for their friend.

"Jacqui! I've been waiting for you," Hannah exclaimed as soon as she spotted her blonde friend.

Jacqui paused outside the classroom door, offering a tentative smile.

"What for? Is everything ok?"

"It's improving... mum and dad had a *big* discussion last night about their finances and toward the end they got me to sit down and talk with them. Mum showed me this," Hannah said, holding out Jacqui's list of ideas regarding cutting costs with Jasper.

Jacqui blushed.

"Mum asked me to write that down, so I did," she mumbled, groping for an excuse.

She knew the last time she had discussed the idea with Hannah; her friend had been far from happy.

"I'm glad you did!" Hannah responded as she headed into the classroom, Jacqui following her.

"It's showing my parents one way to cut back on the costs that are linked to owning Jasper. They told me that because of *my list for Jasper*," she quoted her parents, "that they would each make a list too, trying to match the amount that could be saved in areas that relate to their lives. Apparently your mum already showed my mum how money could be saved on some bills. Suddenly they're both excited about being able to control their finances and keep an eye on our budget."

Jacqui processed all of this as she put her backpack away and sat down at the table. *Lord, I think you just answered my prayer.*

"So... will that solve the problem?" she asked anxiously, glancing up when Geordie bounded through the door.

Hannah nodded enthusiastically.

"It sounds like it! Mum told me that *if* she and dad are able to save as much as I can, because of your list, then things will be looking positive. Apparently they will be in a position where they're earning more than they spend. Then over time they can pay off things that they owe money on and that'll help heaps," she explained, causing Jacqui to grin.

"Alright!" Geordie cheered as she heard the end of the conversation.

She quickly sat down at the table with the other two girls. Hannah looked up at her friend and rolled her eyes.

"What? It sounds like Jacqui to the rescue, to me!" Geordie declared with a grin, earning a laugh from Hannah.

Jacqui blushed.

"I don't know about that... but you helped me to work out the cost of lessons and how much would be saved if Hannah could get free lessons... And it was Kara who agreed to give free lessons," she reminded them quickly.

"Ok, ok. Jacqui, Kara and myself to the rescue!" Geordie amended her previous statement.

With a little help from God. Jacqui grinned at the thought.

"And Mrs. King," Hannah added to the list.

Geordie raised her brows in surprise.

"Huh? What did I miss?" she asked.

Hannah grinned as she repeated the conversation she'd just had with Jacqui. Jacqui sat quietly, barely listening.

A large grin was making its way onto her face as she considered how the situation appeared to be turning around. She thanked God that things were looking positive. She knew that Hannah's parents still needed to find a way to make some changes, but she was glad that Hannah already had a way to save on the costs related to owning Jasper. It looked like her friend was going to get to keep her pony!

Things are fixed, not broken anymore... She glanced at her two friends happily chatting and smiled again. Caitlin and Amelia soon joined the other three and turned the topic elsewhere.

Jacqui's thoughts were interrupted as their teacher arrived in the classroom, gaining everyone's attention. She quickly called the roll and set a group task for them to work on.

"The end of the school year is fast approaching and I think we need to consider what project we can do as a class for our Christmas break up! So I want you to consider if we'll have a morning tea at recess or a lunch time celebration and what topic we might have for the event. I'd like to encourage everyone to dress up for the event, so think of something that people can use as a theme to dress up," Mrs. Hook informed the class.

"So! You can talk with the people on your table and write down at least two ideas for a theme as well as your preference over what time we do the event. This afternoon we'll write up all the theme ideas on the board and then vote for our favourite. The highest number of votes will be our theme for in a couple of weeks' time."

Geordie grinned as she looked at her friends.

"Lunch is surely the best time! It goes for longer," she commented, earning agreeing nods from her friends.

"So... would horses be ok as a theme?" she asked, earning a laugh from Hannah.

Jacqui shook her head.

"What if we suggested animals? Then each of us can think about something horse related, but other people could choose different animals to dress up as," she suggested.

"Brilliant!" Geordie exclaimed, writing it down on a piece of paper.

Caitlin and Amelia were able to quickly suggest some ideas that *weren't* horse related. The five young girls spent the rest of the allotted time debating *which* of the other topics they should nominate as their second idea.

In the end they decided to write them all down. Their teacher had already indicated that once each table had determined at least two topics, they would vote as a class to determine the winning theme. Geordie was quick to point out that their teacher hadn't set a *maximum* number of theme ideas, so the girls were happy to create a long list. As their teacher was indicating that they should finish writing their theme ideas, Jacqui wrote a last word down on their list. Hannah frowned as she read it.

"Broken?" she asked, confused.

Jacqui nodded slowly, feeling her face grow warm.

"I don't get it," Hannah declared.

"I love it!" Geordie exclaimed.

Caitlin and Amelia looked at Geordie in surprise.

"What's so great about something that's broken?"

"Well… it can be fixed. And there are lots of things that are broken that can still be used. It's maybe a weird theme topic to suggest, but there are lots of things we could dress up as…"

"Such as?" Caitlin challenged, her brows raised in disbelief.

"Well…" Geordie stalled, thinking of examples.

"Broken clothes that have holes in them; broken arms or legs; a broken heart" Hannah responded, causing Jacqui to smile thankfully at her friend.

Hannah may not have understood at first, but she was catching on quick. In the end the girls agreed that it was an unusual theme idea, but they would leave it on the list and see what the class thought.

That afternoon when Jacqui arrived home from school she was bursting to share Hannah's news with her mother. She smiled when she realised her mum was already home from work. Her enthusiasm was quickly overridden by curiosity as she spied two small ponies grazing in the quarantine paddock.

One looked to be a black Shetland and the other was a beautiful palomino pony. Jacqui paused outside the gate, watching the two. The black gelding gave her a quick look before busily turning his attention back to the grass before him. He pulled the green plant from the ground in quick bursts. Jacqui smiled as she watched him.

I'm not sure you're even chewing that before you swallow!

Although the pony appeared hungry, he didn't look to be underweight. She wondered if the eager eating was typical of his character. Her attention was soon drawn to the palomino mare as she trotted toward Jacqui at the gate.

Her white mane lifted in the breeze and she stepped high with her front legs. Jacqui's eyes widened as she took in the high stepping trot. *Wow! I wonder what type of pony you are.*

The mare looked to be around 12 hands high, maybe a little more. Jacqui hadn't seen a pony like her before. The palomino stopped just before the gate and stretched out her nose slowly, blowing air through her nostrils. Jacqui grinned, but refrained from touching the horse. The weather was wonderful and she wanted to give Jaq a ride shortly. Although these two ponies looked healthy, she knew they were in the quarantine paddock for a reason. It was better to play it safe and not touch them for now and potentially pass something onto Jaq when she rode him.

"I'll see you two later! You're a very pretty girl," she told the palomino before she turned around and jogged up the driveway.

Jacqui soon learned from her mother about the two ponies. They were being leased by two young girls whose mother had inquired about agistment at Genesis not too long ago. Although they were supposed to turn up at the property the weekend before, the girl's mother had struggled to organise transport for the ponies.

Jacqui remembered that her mother had mentioned the girls were eight and nine years old and new to horse riding and care. She looked forward to meeting them in the near future.

"That's great that we have another two paying clients!" she declared, suddenly thinking about the Johnston's financial situation.

"It is honey. God is providing a little more for us and I'm thankful. How was your day?"

Jacqui grinned and told her mum about her surprise at finding Hannah waiting for her outside the classroom that morning. As she explained about the list that Hannah showed her and Hannah's parents' excitement over controlling their finances Kate's small smile turned into a large grin.

71

"That's such wonderful news, darling. It looks like God's providing some much needed guidance and encouragement for the Johnston's, too."

Jacqui nodded.

"I guess so! He's definitely answered my prayer for Hannah... I wasn't sure how things were going to turn around and she seemed so sad... and even angry with me."

"It can be hard to watch a friend have what you think you're going to lose," Kate agreed with a nod.

"Well I'm glad it's not happening! I'm going to go for a ride on Jaq before dinner," she declared as she headed down toward her bedroom to change.

"Have a great ride, darling," Kate called after her.

Jacqui had no doubt that she would. With the day she'd had, the best way to end it would be a lovely canter through the paddock on her beautiful grey pony.

Ten

Hannah and Jacqui had their first riding lesson together with Kara teaching them that week. Jacqui had wondered what Kara was going to focus on for them in the lesson. She was aware that Hannah was a more accomplished rider than she was.

She was curious, but hadn't given the idea much thought. Her time had been taken up with school, riding and helping Hannah to work out other ways they could save money with regards to Jasper.

Kate King had created a list of things that she wanted completed over the next month to cover Jasper's agistment bill. She had decided after a discussion with the three girls that she and Tony would create a list at the start of each calendar month and it was up to the girls to work out *when* they would do each task. The one rule was that the list needed to be complete *before* the end of that month. Jacqui, Geordie and Hannah had eagerly accepted the terms. Then together they'd decided to dedicate at least one afternoon a week toward doing these tasks – even if it was on a weekend.

Now Jacqui and Hannah were warming up at a walk in the arena paddock. They were circling around Kara who was standing in the middle of the arena as she outlined what she wanted them to do for the lesson.

"Now I know that both of you enjoy jumping! We can do a lot to improve *how* we jump on our horses, without necessarily needing to jump *high*. So today we're going to work on riding broken lines."

Jacqui was surprised as the word broken came up again in her life. She thought it was incredible that she could find so many different ways to describe something as broken. A few weeks ago she wouldn't have given the word much thought. Now it seemed to be involved in every part of her life – riding, horse training, church, her friends and school.

"Can either of you tell me what a broken line is? Or a bending line?" Kara asked the girls as they changed direction at a walk.

"I think I know what a bending line is…" Hannah said as she made sure Jasper was moving forward at an even pace.

Kara nodded at her.

"I'd love to hear your thoughts, Hannah."

"Well… it's where two jumps are to be ridden one after the other, but it's not a straight line from one to the next. There are a set number of strides between the two, but you have to ride around a bend to get to the second one, I think."

"Great! Jacqui, did you follow that explanation?" Kara asked, turning her attention to the blonde on her grey pony.

Jacqui nodded her head, but kept watching where she was going.

"So the difference between a bending line in jumping and a broken line is that the broken line has two jumps that are *at right angles* to each other. This is a 90 degree angle... so if you think about the hands on a clock for when the time is 3 o'clock, where do the hands sit?" she asked, causing Jacqui to look across at her in surprise.

She couldn't see how telling the time was relevant to a jumping lesson. Still, she decided to answer Kara.

"One is at the 12 and the other is at the 3," she replied.

"Great! Now imagine the hands as two different jumps. One jump is sitting at the 12 and the other is around at the 3. We need to be able to guide our horses first over the jump that is at the 12, looking straight ahead and focused on this, but as we land, we need to be focused on *turning* our horses around toward the 3 so that they are heading toward that to jump it next."

Jacqui thought this sounded simple in theory, but knew it would be challenging. It was easier to focus on the next jump when it was straight in front of you after the first. Having to go around a corner or an arc of a circle would be a big challenge!

"Now that we've discussed the idea of a broken line, we'd better get these ponies warmed up! We can get back to the jumping topic in a little bit. How about you two girls ask your ponies to trot for me. Make sure you're on the correct diagonal," Kara instructed, her attention on the two riders trotting around her.

Jacqui glanced down at the outside shoulder of Jaq as he trotted along briskly. She saw that she was rising and falling in time with his outside foreleg moving forward and back. This indicated she was on the correct diagonal and didn't need to change it. She grinned and kept trotting the circle.

After a couple of laps Kara had the two girls changing their direction across the middle of the arena. With Hannah leading, the pair cut across the arena at the letter F, sat for two beats in the middle of the arena and then continued on at a trot until they reached the letter H. Here they turned right and continued trotting in the other direction. After a couple of laps at the trot where Kara had them doing some sitting trot, she encouraged each of the girls to have a canter down the long side of the arena.

Once both pairs of riders and their ponies were well warmed up, Kara instructed the girls to come back to a walk on a loose rein. As they did so, she carried some poles into the arena and set these up on the ground at right angles to each other but with a good spacing between them.

Kara informed the girls that broken lines could be a lot closer together, but this was at a much higher level of riding. For now she wanted the two girls to get the idea of how to ride a broken line, without it being too difficult!

Once Kara was happy with the positioning of the two lots of two poles she had set out in the arena, she encouraged both girls to shorten their stirrups a couple of holes for jumping. They then picked up a trot under her direction and rose into *two point*, their jumping position.

Jacqui found herself momentarily distracted as she spied two figures out walking in the house paddock. She

76

grinned when she realised it was her mother with Dianne. Hannah had told her that afternoon that Dianne was giving up her tennis lessons to cut back on spending. Instead, she was taking Kate up on her offer to go out walking on the property whilst Hannah had her riding lesson with Jacqui.

It seemed a good alternative. It would definitely be cheaper to walk at Genesis!

"I think I've lost you, Jacqui! Jaq seems like he's ready to go over these poles, but are you?" Kara called out, gaining the young girl's attention.

The blonde rider blushed.

"Sorry, Kara! I'm ready."

Under the older girl's direction Hannah and Jacqui each rode the two sets of broken lines at first a walk and a trot. When they were comfortable with this, Kara asked if they were up for a canter. The two girls nodded enthusiastically.

"Ok. This is where you're really going to have to concentrate! I want you to treat the poles like a jump, rising into your jumping position over them, looking toward the second jump *and* counting the number of strides that you do between each jump. Got it?"

At another pair of affirming nods, Kara directed Jacqui to come and stand in the middle of the arena with her, whilst Hannah rode the two lots of poles at opposite ends of the arena. Then it would be Jacqui's turn.

Half an hour later both girls had a lot to think about. They'd each gotten plenty of practice over the two lots of poles that Kara had later turned into cross bar jumps for them. Jacqui felt the lesson had been a very challenging one – she had a lot to work on! But she was grinning as she and Hannah rode their ponies on a loose rein at a walk outside the arena as they cooled down. Kara was busy putting the poles back where they belonged.

"Thanks so much for allowing me to ride in Jacqui's lesson, Kara," Hannah said shyly as the girls continued at a sedate walk.

"That's fine, Hannah! It's great practice for me and I'm already teaching Jacqui, so it doesn't take extra time.

"Oh, Jacqui, did I tell you that your new client with the two daughters who are leasing ponies has contacted me about teaching her girls? They're having their first lesson next week. I've already checked with your mum and it's ok for me to teach them at Genesis, too. Then we can use the arena and their ponies don't have to come over to my parents' place."

Jacqui beamed.

"That sounds great!"

"I'm excited, too," Kara responded as she finished putting the poles away.

She said a quick goodbye to the girls, indicating that she needed to ride her mare Phoenix before getting stuck into some homework. Jacqui and Hannah waved goodbye before they turned their attention back to finishing their ride.

Jacqui looked out over the property as they made their way back toward the tie up area. The grass was turning a yellow colour with the summer heat and sun, but it still looked beautiful to Jacqui. She was so thankful to be living on land where they could have horses.

The two girls dismounted, tied their ponies up with a quick release knot and started to remove their riding gear.

"I thought I was going to lose all of this," Hannah mused as she put Jasper's saddle on a rail.

Jacqui nodded slowly, thinking.

"I thought you might, too… but worst of all, I thought I was losing a friend," she said quietly as she ran a curry comb over Jaq's back where the saddle had been sitting.

In time she looked toward Hannah and found her friend staring back at her.

"What do you mean?" Hannah asked quizzically.

Jacqui shrugged.

"It seemed… that because you were going to lose Jasper you were angry; especially with me… And I thought that if you lost him, that you wouldn't want to spend time with me anymore," she confided.

Hannah frowned and turned her attention back to brushing her bay gelding. Jacqui wondered if she'd just made the girl angry again.

"I'm sorry, Jacqui. That wasn't fair of me. I was scared – and angry! But it wasn't right to get angry at you because, well," she gestured out across the property that the King family owned.

Jacqui nodded.

"I love this place and I'm so glad we can all ride here… but even if one of us couldn't have a pony for some reason, I don't want it to stop us spending time together.

You two didn't stop spending time with me when I didn't have Matty," she reminded Hannah.

Hannah nodded enthusiastically.

"That's true! I think we should make it a rule that if any of us doesn't have a pony *for any reason* that we still make an effort to spend time here with each other and the others' ponies."

"I love it. Let's tell Geordie tomorrow," Jacqui suggested with a smile.

The girls were just finishing up with their ponies when Kate and Dianne came in from their walk. Jacqui shot her mum a quick smile.

"We'll just put them out in the paddock," she informed the two women.

Kate nodded and sat on an upturned bucket in the tie up area. Dianne inspected another bucket before glancing down at her matching walking outfit. She opted to stand and wait for the girls.

A few minutes later the two returned and Dianne and Hannah said goodbye. Kate grinned as she watched their car head down the driveway, a trail of dust behind it.

"How was your ride?" she asked Jacqui as they walked toward the house.

"Great! And I think things are all ok with Hannah, now. We… had a good talk and decided that if any one of us is without a pony, it won't affect our friendship."

"That sounds like a wonderful decision," Kate replied as they left their shoes at the door and headed inside.

"How was your walk?" Jacqui asked curiously.

"Really good! It was a great chance to get to know Dianne on a deeper level. I even had the chance to invite her and her family along to church on the weekend. She seemed unsure, but said she would talk it over with Michael."

Jacqui's brows rose at this information. She couldn't imagine Hannah coming along to church. Kate laughed.

"They don't have to say yes, Jacqui. But they'll never have the opportunity to do so if I don't ask. Dianne is already aware that we hold God in high regard in our family. It wouldn't hurt for her to know that we also value going to church on Sundays. If the Johnston's decide to come to church, that would be wonderful."

In the end Jacqui agreed that it would. She headed to the bathroom to clean up before dinner, thankful that her mum had prepared something in advance for that evening. She was more than ready to eat when her father got home!

Eleven

Friday of that week came by quickly. Jacqui knew she had another lesson with Jared and this time she looked forward to it. She had been thankful for the boy's insight with regards to Hannah the week before and felt the whole situation had well and truly turned around. It seemed that Jared remembered the discussion, too. After saying hello he asked how Hannah was doing.

"Great! Things have changed for the better," Jacqui smiled as they walked together out to the arena paddock.

"Awesome. What happened?" Jared asked as he walked beside her.

Jacqui detailed how she and Geordie had worked out a list of things that could be cheaper with regards to owning Jasper. She said that once Hannah's parents saw this, they were motivated to make their own lists.

"And now things are looking better *plus* Hannah gets to keep Jasper," Jacqui concluded proudly.

"That really is great," Jared said as he stood on the mounting block to get on Captain.

Jacqui nodded and looked up at the young boy in surprise. She smiled broadly and he raised his brows in question.

"I just realised, Jared. I took your advice... about praying," she clarified as he looked confused, "and I honestly think that's what has made all the difference."

Jared grinned as he asked Captain to walk around the edge of the arena.

"That's pretty cool," he said honestly.

Jacqui agreed that it was. She realised with a start that it felt nice to be talking with him about God and praying. She wondered if that would ever be the case with Hannah.

"So! Can you remind me what we covered last week?" she prompted her student.

Jared gave her a quick rundown of the lesson they had had the Friday before. Jacqui nodded as he talked about the trotting he'd gotten to do on Captain.

"So... I was reading this book," he said hesitantly.

Jacqui nodded for him to continue.

"It was about riding," he admitted, causing her to smile, "and it said that you should rise to a particular *diagonal* when trotting. What's that?"

Jacqui beamed; glad she could answer the question. She was also pleased that Jared wanted to learn more about riding and was taking the initiative to read.

"I have lots of horse books if you want to borrow any," she offered quickly.

Jared nodded enthusiastically as he changed direction and started walking Captain around the arena on the other rein.

"So I've learned that when a horse trots, their legs move in diagonal pairs. The front left and back right hind leg step off the ground together and touch the ground together," Jacqui explained slowly.

At Jared's affirming nod she continued.

"And it's the same for the right front leg and the back left leg. These are diagonal pairs of legs that work together. So this is the diagonal that the book is talking about… when you ride the trot and rise to it, you're rising up and down with one particular pair of diagonal legs."

"Cool! But… how do you tell which one to go with?" he asked, bringing Captain to a stop at the letter A before asking him to walk on again after a few seconds.

Jacqui had told him to stop at every second letter to make sure that Captain was listening to him.

"I don't think it matters when you're going in a straight line… but when you're riding a circle or in an arena, then you should be following the pattern of the outside front leg. I think I've been told that this helps the horse to balance better when trotting around corners," Jacqui informed him.

Jared nodded as he processed this.

"So… because I am riding clockwise at the moment," he said slowly, thinking, "I need to rise with the left front leg?"

"Perfect! So when Captain's leg moves *forward* at the trot, you should be *rising* out of the saddle."

"Ok, I think I understand. One more question though."

Jacqui nodded for him to keep talking.

84

"If I'm *not* doing that, how do I change it?"

Jacqui laughed in delight, glad she could answer that question too.

"You just need to sit for two beats in the saddle. So instead of rising, you sit one extra beat *and then* rise. That'll put you on the opposite diagonal to what you were rising to before."

Jared beamed at the explanation.

"Looks like you've got that idea. Will we do some trotting?" Jacqui asked.

Jared didn't need to be asked twice. He eagerly shortened up his reins and applied pressure with his calves. Captain moved out into a steady trot and soon the young boy was rising up and down in time to the two beat gait. Once he seemed steady, Jacqui encouraged him to glance down at Captain's shoulder.

When Jared did so, he told Jacqui that he thought he was on the correct diagonal. Jacqui confirmed that he was before encouraging him to sit for two beats. He did so, confused.

"Why would I want to be on the *wrong* one?" he asked curiously.

"Just so you know what it looks and feels like," Jacqui responded cheerily.

She got Jared to look down again and he confirmed that he could see he wasn't on the correct diagonal. Jacqui had him sit for another two beats to correct the issue.

Half an hour later the two finished up their lesson. Jared was beaming as they walked back toward the tie up area.

"I feel so much more confident at the trot *and* I now know how to tell if I'm rising correctly," he said proudly.

Jacqui grinned.

"It's pretty cool, isn't it? I love that there's so much to learn about horses and riding... I don't think I will ever stop learning about them."

"Could you imagine if you knew as much about horses as God did?" Jared asked suddenly, causing Jacqui to pause in surprise.

She helped Jared to secure Captain with a head collar and lead rope as she thought about this. She had never considered that idea before. She noted with a smile that Jared loosened the girth and secured it in the stirrup iron before removing the saddle. He was learning quickly.

"I don't think I could imagine that," she finally responded, "it would be incredible though, I'm sure."

Jared nodded as he sorted through the bucket of brushes beside him. He pulled out a rubber curry comb and started to brush out the sweat from Captain's coat. Although they had only walked and trotted in their lesson, it was a warm afternoon and the older gelding had felt it.

Jacqui observed Jared as he finished brushing down Captain. Happy that he seemed to know what he was doing, she let her mind wander. The following Monday at school the students would find out what their topic would be for the end of year break up. Jacqui was looking forward to it.

Suddenly the word broken came to mind and she thought of her four friends at school. As an idea formed, she grinned at the thought. *If that theme does get chosen, I'm so talking to the girls about a costume idea!*

Jacqui was pleased for the lesson that she'd had recently on the word broken. She felt it had applied to her life over the past few weeks in so many different ways. What was even more pleasing was that now *nothing* felt broken. Things appeared to be fixed and all where they should be. She prayed it would continue that way.

About the Author

Christine Meunier considers herself introduced to the wonderful world of horses at the late age of 13 when her parents agreed to lease a horse for her. She started experiencing horses via books from a young age and continues to do so, but recognises that horses cannot be learnt solely from books.

She has been studying horses from age 16, starting with the Certificate II in Horse Studies. She completed the Bachelor of Equine Science in 2015.

Christine has worked at numerous thoroughbred studs in Australia as well as overseas in Ireland for a breeding season.

She then gained experience in a couple of Melbourne based horse riding schools, instructing at a basic level before heading off overseas again, this time to South Africa to spend hours in the saddle of endurance and trail horses on the Wild Coast.

Particularly passionate about the world of breeding horses, she writes a blog about equine education which you can view at http://equus-blog.com/

You can contact Christine via email at christine@christinemeunierauthor.com.

Sign up to her author news and receive updates – and freebies – as they are available! http://eepurl.com/bAiMpL

Every effort is made to ensure that this book is free of spelling and grammatical errors. That said, I am only human! If you find any errors, I'd love to know so that I can correct them. You can contact me at christine@christinemeunierauthor.com with details of any issues you may find.

Made in the USA
Coppell, TX
30 January 2020